Published in Great Britain in 2002 by Hodder Wayland,
an imprint of Hodder Children's Books

British Library Cataloguing in Publication Data
Tonge, Neil
Freedom song : the story of Nelson Mandela.
- (Historical storybooks)
1.Mandela, Nelson, 1918- 2.Historical fiction
3.Children's stories
I.Title II.Morris, Tony
823.9'14[J]

ISBN 0-7502-3905-0

Printed in Hong Kong by Wing King Tong Co. Ltd.

Hodder Children's Books,
A division of Hodder Headline Limited,
338 Euston Road,
London NW1 3BH

Freedom Song

The Story of Nelson Mandela

Neil Tonge

Illustrated by Tony Morris

an imprint of Hodder Children's Books

Nelson Mandela (1918-)

1918 Nelson Mandela was born in the Transkei, South Africa, on 18 July.

1939 He entered university at Fort Hare.

1942 Nelson started studying law at Witswatersand University.

1943 He helped found the African National Congress.

1951 Mandela qualified as a lawyer.

1956 Five years later he stood trial, accused of treason.

1960 The Sharpeville Massacre took place.

1961 Mandela was arrested but then released. A year later, in 1962, he was imprisoned.

1990 He was released from prison on 11 February.

1994 Nelson Mandela was elected president after the first free and fair elections in South Africa's history.

Chapter 1
'It was an Accident'

'Syabonga!'

Syabonga stopped weeding the flower bed and looked up. It was nearly midday and he had to shield his eyes from the glare of the sun.

'Look what I have!' Kris Hope, the ten-year-old son of Syabonga's employer, bounded across the emerald green lawn, swerving at the last minute to avoid the lawn sprinklers that sent a constant spray of liquid diamonds into the air.

Kris's face beamed with joy as he thrust his new Gameboy into Syabonga's hands. 'What do you think of this? Isn't it neat?'

Syabonga propped his hoe against a jacaranda bush, slightly crushing the beautiful purple flowers, and took the Gameboy from Kris.

'Master Hope, please. I must not stop.
Your father will be angry.' Syabonga was
only three years older, but Kris came from
the world of the wealthy white families that
ruled South Africa, while he came from the
poor black townships that ringed the city
of Johannesburg.

'Oh, just hold it a minute. No one will know,' Kris insisted.

Syabonga quickly looked around. There was no one in sight and the jacaranda bush hid them both from anyone in the house. Syabonga's fingers trembled. This would take several months of his wages to buy, even if – in his wildest dreams – he could ever think of buying one. His wages were needed by his mother, back in the township of Alexandra, a vast sprawl of single-room corrugated iron shacks.

'Kris, what does this do?'
Syabonga turned the
Gameboy toward his
young friend.

'Here! Here! Press this,'
Kris said, with a mixture of
excitement and irritation.
As the younger boy
grabbed for the computer
game, it slipped from
Syabonga's grasp and
crashed onto the drive,
the case splitting in
an ugly crack. Both
boys stepped back,
horrified.

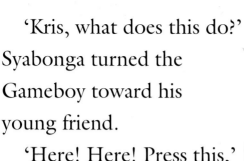

As they stared at the broken case in disbelief, the voice of Kris's father boomed out from behind the bush. He'd been walking back down the drive with a bundle of letters in his hand when he'd heard the crash.

'Kris! What's going on?' He looked down at the shattered computer game and up into Syabonga's face.

'Dad, Dad it was an acc...' Kris attempted to explain but his voice trailed away in a stammer as his father ordered him back to the house.

'I'll talk to you later. I've told you before, Syabonga is paid to work here, not to play.'

Kris bowed his head and gingerly picked up the shattered case. Slowly and miserably he made his way back to the house, disappearing into the shadow that hung over the veranda.

Dr Alan Hope turned to face Syabonga. His face was stern.

'Syabonga, I am very disappointed in you. I have given you and your uncle work here. You have regular money. I will have to see if I can keep you. This is not the first time...'

There was nothing Syabonga could do or say. Kris's father was angry. If he tried to answer back, he'd be finished and maybe his uncle too.

'Sorry, sir. I did not mean for this to happen.' Syabonga kept his head down, not daring to look at his boss.

'I'm not pleased. I will have to decide what to do.' Syabonga shifted his gaze ever so slightly to look into Dr Hope's face, searching for a flicker of forgiveness. But there was none.

Chapter 2
'Maybe Things will Change'

Syabonga stared at his Uncle Joshua as he sat miserably on a piece of sacking on the floor of their sleeping shack.

'I'm sorry Uncle, but it was not me who was to blame.'

Joshua was annoyed. He didn't want to lose this job. He was fifty and wouldn't be able to find work elsewhere.

'Syabonga, you know the white man is always right, the black man is always wrong! This is the way it is.'

Syabonga hung his head. He just could not accept that life had to be so unfair.

Joshua began to soften. He could see that Syabonga was upset but he couldn't shake from his mind the threat of being thrown out of work.

'Well, after tomorrow… maybe things will change.'

'Tomorrow? Why tomorrow?' Syabonga looked puzzled, and then he remembered. Of course! Nelson Mandela, the leader of the black people in South Africa, would be released from prison after twenty-eight long years.

Hope welled up inside Syabonga. Things would get better. Once Mandela was free, the separation of white and black people would come to an end and everyone would be treated fairly in a new South Africa.

Although he knew the story of Mandela's struggle well, he never tired of hearing it.

'Uncle, tell me again. Tell me the story of Mandela.'

Joshua leaned back on his bunk, his hands resting behind his head.

Chapter 3
Son of a Chief

'You know Nelson Mandela was no ordinary boy,' Joshua began. 'He was the son of a royal chief from the Transkei born long ago in 1918. But, although he was a chief's son, he wasn't too important to do the ordinary things that all boys in the countryside did – herd the cattle and sheep and help with the farming.'

Syabonga's eyes widened in wonder. 'You mean he did not have a life of ease, even though he was a chief's son!'

Joshua smiled, and then looked more serious as he continued. 'But when Nelson was only twelve his life changed for ever. His father became seriously ill. Before the chief died he asked his paramount chief to look after the boy, for he realized that his son had special qualities of leadership.

'The paramount chief paid for Nelson to go to a mission school. And it was there that Nelson first came to realize that white people had all the power in South Africa.

'The history books at the school only described white heroes and talked about black people as if we were children who needed to be civilized. He learned how the Dutch and British settlers had come to this part of Africa during the seventeenth century and had defeated the blacks.

'Over the years the all-white government had become more extreme, passing laws that kept us as labourers and servants. We were not allowed to move freely around the country and were forced to live in "homelands".'

'That's the same as now isn't it, Uncle?' Syabonga interrupted.

'Yes. Still the same but not for long we hope,' nodded Joshua, before continuing.

'Even though Nelson did not agree with many of the books he read, he did well at school and went on to university at Fort Hare. But he was already beginning to think about ways of changing things. He soon got into trouble for leading a protest at the poor conditions black people were forced to live in.

'When he returned home his chief was angry and ordered him to give up the protest. Nelson refused. Then, when the chief set about arranging a marriage for him, he ran off to lose himself in the big city of Johannesburg.'

Syabonga's mouth fell open at the thought of disobeying a chief. 'That must have meant trouble for him,' he breathed.

'Yes, it did,' answered Joshua. 'The chief was furious but Nelson did not want to be pushed into doing things he did not agree with. If he'd only known, his troubles were just beginning…

'Like all of us black South Africans, Nelson needed a permit to work, to live in a township and to travel – because of the pass laws. Life was hard. Mandela was tall and strong and took on a job as a guard at a goldmine. At that time he was living in Alexandra – our home township – and there he met Walter Sisulu, who became his lifelong friend. He persuaded Nelson to continue his law studies at the university.'

Chapter 4
On Trial

Syabonga rubbed his eyes. He was exhausted but he wanted to hear more about his hero. 'What about the struggle, Uncle?' he asked eagerly. 'How did Nelson become our leader?'

Joshua was also tired but he wanted his nephew to know the truth. The old man drank some water from a tin mug, cleared his throat and continued.

'Nelson was not content to be a lawyer. He and a student friend, Oliver Tambo, joined the African National Congress (ANC), which was fighting for better treatment of black people in South Africa. He soon became one of its leaders at a time when life was getting even more difficult for us. The government wanted to separate blacks and whites completely. Its word for this was apartheid.

'Nelson and the other ANC leaders hated apartheid because it meant that we black people were not allowed to live in certain areas, could not vote, and could not send our children to the same schools as white people. We were not allowed to go to the same shops or even sit on the same park benches.

'Nelson and the other leaders organized many demonstrations, particularly against the pass laws. In Johannesburg, Mandela made a speech at a meeting which went on beyond 11p.m., the curfew. (After the curfew we Africans needed a special pass to be out.) As they left the hall his supporters were arrested.

'Singing the ANC anthem *Nkosi Sikelel' iAfrica* ("Lord Bless Africa"), they were bundled into police vans and driven away to jail. During the next four months more than 8,500 volunteers went to jail. Among them were a few white people who agreed with the demonstrations. But the publicity was good for the ANC and many thousands flocked to join.

'Now the police started to watch them closely,' said Joshua, frowning at the memory. 'At first Nelson was banned, which meant he couldn't go to any public meetings and he was only allowed to meet one person at a time.

'Then, at dawn on 5 December 1956, there was a loud banging on Nelson's front door.

"Maak oop!" ("Open up, police!")

'All over South Africa, hundreds of men and women, black and white, were being arrested, and 150 – including the leaders of the ANC – were charged with treason. The penalty for treason was death.

'When the trial opened in Johannesburg the streets were full of supporters singing freedom songs. But the government had not thought about the case carefully enough, and Mandela and the other prisoners were given bail.'

'What did that mean?' asked Syabonga.

'It meant they were free to live at home during the trial,' his uncle explained.

'So in between his appearance at the courts Nelson was able to carry on his work with the ANC. He always said the ANC was not protesting against whites but against unjust laws, and they were determined to protest peacefully.'

Chapter 5
On the Run

Joshua braced his aching shoulders against the metal bunk. He was nearing the end of the story.

'The trial went on for four years and the world outside South Africa heard about Mandela and the other leaders of the ANC. When Harold Macmillan, the British Prime Minister, visited in February 1960, he shocked all the white people by telling them that a "wind of change" was sweeping through the whole of Africa.

'A few weeks later at Sharpeville – you know, that township south of Johannesburg – the police opened fire into a crowd of black people peacefully protesting against the pass laws. That was a terrible day for our people. Sixty-nine were killed and nearly 200 wounded, many of them women and children. Photographs of parents carrying their dead children away from the scene of the massacre were on the front pages of newspapers all over the world.

'At last, after four and a half years, on 29 March 1961, Mandela stood in the dock with the other accused.

'The judge passed sentence. "You are found not guilty. You may go."

'They looked at one another in disbelief, then smiled and left the court. But their joy didn't last long. The government banned the ANC as an illegal organization. But this was not going to stop Mandela. He went "underground", disguising himself and living like an outlaw.

'On 5 August, after seventeen months on the run, he was finally captured.

'Just before he was sentenced the judge allowed Nelson to speak. He spoke for nearly four hours, carefully explaining his beliefs. His words echoed around the world. I still remember what he said.

'"Whites tend to regard Africans as a separate breed. They do not look upon them as people with families of their own; they do not realize that they have emotions – that they fall in love like white people do; that they want to be with their wives and children; that they want to earn enough money to support their families, to feed and clothe them and send them to school. And what house boy or garden boy or labourer can ever hope to do that?"

'But the judge was unmoved. Nelson was sentenced to life imprisonment.

'For twenty-eight long years, he remained in prison, hardly ever seeing his wife or children. But South Africa and the world did not forget him. The townships burst into riots. The police and the army poured in, shooting and arresting the protesters. Everywhere people were inspired by Nelson Mandela. Boycotts of South African goods and sporting teams cut our country off from the rest of the world. By the 1980s, the white South African government knew that they had to release Mandela or face ruin.

'And tomorrow, Syabonga,' finished his uncle triumphantly, 'is the day we have been waiting for, for so long!'

Syabonga stretched wearily.

Tomorrow, he thought, tomorrow… Would tomorrow be any better? He would have to face Dr Hope, and perhaps he and his uncle would lose their jobs?

Chapter 6
'All the Yesterdays'

'Come, Syabonga. Come to the house.'

Kris was shouting excitedly, waving his hands in the air.

Syabonga feared the worst. His skin prickled. How would he explain to his family that he had lost his job?

'Go in. My dad's in the front room.' Kris pushed Syabonga on his way. As a garden boy he wasn't usually invited into the house. He wiped his feet and headed for the front entrance.

When Syabonga shuffled into the living room the television was flickering in the corner. There were crowds of people on the screen and they were all straining forward to see two lone figures striding down a long, dusty road.

Almost absent-mindedly, Dr Hope turned to Syabonga. 'That's Nelson Mandela and his wife Winnie.'

Then he seemed to collect his thoughts and looked directly at the boy. 'About yesterday. I'm sorry for losing my temper. Kris has told me what happened. I want you to stay and work here.'

On the screen, Nelson Mandela had reached the gates of the prison and the crowd had broken into the beautiful, swelling notes of the ANC anthem *Nkosi Sikelel' iAfrica*.

Then Dr Hope muttered, more to himself than to Syabonga, 'All the yesterdays... I'm sorry for all the yesterdays.'

Syabonga stared at the television screen. After twenty-eight years, Nelson was an *old* man. He'd expected a warrior, a fighter – he'd expected to see someone *young*.

Yet, despite all he had suffered, Mandela was smiling. Not just because he'd been released but because he realized that this was the beginning of change – the change he'd spent his whole life working for.

Chapter 7
A New South Africa

On Sunday, 11 February 1990, Nelson
Mandela strode out of prison. He was an
old man of seventy-one, though still fit.

In the months that followed he began
talks with President F.W. de Klerk. A new
system of government was agreed, based
upon a vote for each adult. Apartheid was
swept away. In April 1994, the first free
democratic elections in South Africa's
history made Nelson Mandela the new
president.

Glossary

apartheid a system of government in South Africa, which completely separated black and white people

bail a sum of money paid so that a person doesn't have to stay in jail

banned forbidden to attend meetings and to travel

boycotts refusing to buy certain goods or services

curfew a time after which it is forbidden to be out on the streets

democracy a system of government that gives equal voting rights to all people in a country

elections democratically choosing the leaders of a country by voting for them

homelands tribal lands in South Africa which the white South African government claimed were the only settlement areas for black people

massacre the violent killing of a large number of people

mission school a school run by a Christian organization

paramount chief a chief who rules over other chiefs

prejudice dislike of someone purely because of his or her colour or beliefs

president the title of a leader of a country which is a republic (has no royal family)

townships poor areas where black people were allowed to live